The Kite Flyer

and Other Stories

Rosanne Keller

SIGNAL HILL™

PUBLICATIONS

D0943491

ATTENTION READERS: We would like to hear what you think about our books. Please send your comments or suggestions to:

Signal Hill Publications
P.O. Box 131
Syracuse, NY 13210-0131

SIGNAL HILL™

PUBLICATIONS

ISBN 0-88336-560-X

Copyright © 1992
Signal Hill Publications
A publishing imprint of Laubach Literacy International
Box 131, Syracuse, New York 13210-0131

Printed in the United States of America

Illustrated by Cheri Bladholm

9 8 7 6 5 4 3 2

The Kite Flyer

Flyer

and Other Stories

Table of Contents

The
Kite
Flyer

Losing a Job

Anna is in the kitchen crying into a dish towel. She is wearing a blue dress. She wore this dress for her daughter's wedding. Her matching hat lies on the table. Anna loves that hat. She sewed the flowers on it herself, by hand. Her husband, Helmut, walks into the room.

Helmut and Anna have been married for 26 years. Helmut owns the shoe repair shop below their apartment. He works long hours. He even works on Sundays sometimes, when the shop is closed. But today he took the morning off. He and Anna went to their youngest daughter's wedding.

The wedding was very small. It wasn't even in a church. And the bride and groom only wanted their parents there. They didn't invite anyone else.

In the old days, weddings were grander. Anna made herself a special dress for today anyway. The bride and groom were a handsome couple.

And now they were gone.

My life is over, Anna thinks. She isn't thinking of the wedding. She is thinking of seeing her daughter drive away. Her last child has moved away.

This thought makes her cry again.

"Hey," says Helmut from the doorway. "This should be a happy day. Why are you crying?" he asks.

"I've lost my job," cries Anna.

"What?" says Helmut. He laughs. "You never had a job."

Anna raises her head slowly. She looks at Helmut. "Never had a job?" she whispers. "What do you think I was doing all those years?"

Helmut looks surprised. "You stayed home. You took care of our children," he says, "and the house."

"And you don't think that is a job?" Anna wipes her eyes with the dish towel. She doesn't want tears dripping on her new dress.

"You don't understand. All our children are gone," she cries. "Life hasn't changed for you at all. But my life has turned upside down."

"Listen," says Helmut. "Children grow up. They leave home. You've been a good mother. They all turned out fine. Why are you talking about a job, anyway? You don't need a job."

Helmut looks at his watch. "When are we going to have lunch?" he asks. "I have to get back to the shop."

Anna stands up. "Lunch?" she shouts. "Is that all you have to say?" She picks up her hat. "Our youngest child has moved across the United States. And all you think about is eating and work?"

"She's only moved to Kansas," Helmut says. "That's not so far. And I'm hungry."

"Then fix your own lunch!" Anna yells. She slams the door as she runs out of the apartment.

Running Away

Anna runs along the sidewalk. Her blue, high-heeled wedding shoes hurt her feet. Tears stream down her face. She doesn't care anymore if the tears drip on her dress.

Helmut still thinks he is living in the old country, she thinks. Could Helmut fix his own lunch? He has never fixed a meal in his life. That is what wives do.

In the old country, wives didn't go out and work. They stayed home and took care of children. They cooked and washed clothes. They had no choice.

But in the old country, children didn't move away. Children married and still lived close to their parents. Sometimes they even lived at home. They were still part of the family.

This was true when Anna and Helmut
were young. They lived in the same town as
their parents. They broke the tradition when
they moved to America. Life would never be
the same again.

America is so big. Grown-up children in
America almost always move away. All of our
children are scattered like seeds, Anna thinks.
Two in California. Two in Texas. Now the
youngest one will live in Kansas.

Anna loved her life when the children were little. We were so busy all those years, she thinks. Helmut in the shop, me with the children.

Now it's just the two of us. Helmut still has his work. But what will I do, Anna wonders?

Anna sees the park just ahead of her. She used to bring the children to this park. Now she often comes here alone to think.

Anna runs to the edge of the small pond. She is tired from running. She sits on a bench to rest. Breathing hard, she looks across the water. She remembers the children playing there by the pond. "I did what I was supposed to do," she says out loud. "I did my job and I did it happily."

"You did what happily?" says a voice next to her. Anna looks and notices the older woman sitting there. It's Greta. Anna knows her. Greta is also from Germany. She walks her dog in the park every day.

Anna is ashamed that Greta heard her talking to herself. "Hello, Greta," she says. "I'm, uh, just counting my blessings."

"You must have a lot of blessings. You are out of breath," says Greta. She looks at Anna. "What are you running from?"

Anna thinks for a minute. "The future," she says. "I guess I'm running from the future."

The older woman shakes her head. "It's better to turn and face it," she says.

Anna doesn't say anything. She just closes her eyes. But in her mind she doesn't see the future. She sees the past.

She thinks back to the first few years of her marriage.

Anna was 16 when she married Helmut. They lived in East Germany. Things were difficult there. Helmut had to work hard as a shoemaker. He didn't make much money.

In six years, they had five children. Two boys and three girls. Then they came to America. They wanted their children to grow up in a democracy.

Anna takes a deep breath and sighs, remembering.

At first, they had so little. But they were happy. Anna loved being a mother. She did not mind getting up in the night to nurse the children. To bring them water. To kiss away bad dreams. She even enjoyed sewing and taking care of their clothes.

Her favorite memories were of the family meals. Anna loves to cook. The kitchen has always been the heart of their home.

Anna thinks of Helmut. Sometimes he comes into the kitchen while she cooks. He sits and drinks coffee and they talk. Those are some of their best times together.

Meals were noisy when the children were home. They all talked as they ate. Helmut told stories. The children laughed.

"You must be thinking good thoughts," says Greta. "You are smiling."

Anna opens her eyes. "Children need their mothers so much," she says. "Some people think it's a burden. But it's good to be needed."

"And you don't feel needed now," says Greta.

Anna says quietly, "I feel like a mother bird with an empty nest." She looks across the water. Then she frowns. "All my husband wants is his lunch."

"Ah," says Greta. She nods with understanding. Then she says, "We hear a lot about empty nests these days. But life goes on after the children leave."

"Being a mother is such an important job," Anna says. "It's all I've ever done. Now I feel like I've been fired from my job. I don't know how to do anything else. Who am I? Without the children, I'm nobody."

"What about your husband?" asks Greta.

"He works all the time," says Anna. "He only comes upstairs to eat and sleep. He doesn't understand. He thinks like a man from the old country."

Greta gets up to leave. "He *is* a man from the old country," she says.

The Kite

After Greta leaves, Anna sits for a long time. She thinks about Helmut.

In the old country, men were supposed to be as strong as steel. They didn't cry. They didn't show their feelings. Or talk about them.

Greta is right, Anna thinks. Helmut *is* a man from the old country.

Has he also done just what he was supposed to do, Anna wonders? Has he also been happy to do it?

Anna remembers the night when they left East Germany. It was dark when Helmut woke her up. "Come," he said. "Get the children dressed. It's time."

They walked through the night. At the border, Helmut gave the guard a package. After that, the guard pretended he didn't see them walk through. Anna never knew how Helmut did it. She only knew that they had no money when they arrived in America.

Anna looks across the pond. It is as still as a mirror. The trees and the sky are reflected in the water. She walks to the edge. She looks down and sees her face in the water.

Anna picks up a stone. She drops it into the pond. It disappears with a splash. The trees, the sky, and her own face are lost in the ripples.

"This is like life," Anna mutters. "You think everything is clear. Then something happens to confuse it." She watches a long time. The ripples begin to smooth. She begins to see her face again. Then she notices a moving shape reflected in the water.

Anna turns around. Just behind her, someone is flying a red kite. At first she thinks it is a child. But as she looks closer, she sees it is a woman!

The kite dances in the sky. Anna watches the woman holding the string. How surprising! A grown woman flying a kite!

Anything can happen, Anna thinks. Then she laughs. Women don't always have to do just what other people expect.

Anna walks over to the woman. "Could I fly the kite for a moment?" she asks.

Helmut

Helmut just looks at the door after Anna leaves. She never slammed the door before. What is the matter with her?

He goes into the kitchen. It seems empty without Anna. The whole house seems empty. It used to be full of noise and children everywhere. He sits down in the quiet kitchen. It's too quiet. Anna must feel this way, too, he thinks.

Helmut knows where she is. She always goes to the park when she has a problem. He puts on his jacket. He walks out the door. He doesn't slam it. He closes it quietly.

Downstairs, he enters his shop. Several pairs of shoes lie on the counter. He needs to repair them. But the shoes can wait. He finds a piece of cardboard. On it he writes *Closed until Monday*.

Helmut smiles as he puts his sign in the window. He hasn't had a weekend off for a long time. But this weekend, the time off is important.

He walks down to the park. When he walks into the park, he sees Anna. He stops. He can't believe what he sees.

Anna is standing in the grass without her shoes on. Her hat has blown off her head. The wind is catching her blue dress.

She is flying a kite!

As Helmut watches, he feels tears in his eyes. Anna looks more beautiful than ever before.

Anna turns and smiles when she sees Helmut. She hands the kite back to the woman. Then she picks up her shoes. She walks over to Helmut.

"I'm sorry," she says.

"No," Helmut says. "I am the one who is sorry."

"I just feel so useless," says Anna. "Without the children, I don't know what to do. I don't need a job. But I need to be needed."

Helmut looks at her a long time. "You still have me. I need you."

"I know," says Anna. "I was just thinking about that."

Helmut takes Anna's hand. "Come home. I'll fix us some lunch."

Anna stops. She stares at Helmut. "You are going to fix lunch? You have never fixed a meal in your life."

"But I know how," Helmut says.

"When did you learn?" asks Anna.

"All these years I've watched." Helmut winks at Anna. "I've had a very good teacher."

Helmut picks up a flat stone. When he throws it, it skips across the water. Then he speaks again. "And I still have a lot to learn."

Can They Stay?

The Devil's Highway

It is July, 1984. The summer is blazing hot.

Luis has already walked 35 miles. His throat hurts. His eyes burn. He is so thirsty. He reaches for the water bottle tied to his belt. It is empty. How can he go on without water?

The Arizona desert is like an oven. There is no shade. Only cactuses and thin bushes. But Luis and the three other men keep walking.

The sun is like a ball of fire. It burns their necks and their feet. We are not going to get there, Luis thinks. We will die here.

Luis and his three friends left Mexico by moonlight last night. To Luis that seems like years ago.

If they are lucky, they will get to Highway 8. Just north of the highway is a canal with water. That is 40 miles from the Mexican border. Forty miles across a desert. There is no water in this desert.

Many Mexicans cross the border into the United States here. They have one common dream. They want jobs so they can support their families. They walk north across this desert. It is called "the Devil's Highway."

There are many dangers: the heat and the thirst, the border patrol airplanes, the snakes.

The men fear the rattlesnakes. But they fear the border patrol more. If the border patrol finds them, they will have to go back to Mexico.

The worst danger is thirst. If you run out of water too early in the trip, you will die. Luis knows this.

"Stop," says one of the men. "Let's sit down and rest." Luis gets under a bush near the others. Nobody talks. One man passes around his water bottle. They all share the little bit of water. They throw away the empty bottle.

Luis reaches in his pocket. He takes out the picture of his family. There is his wife, Elena, holding little María. Carlos stands proudly beside her. Carlos is five years old. María is two.

Luis holds the picture tightly. He is risking his life for them.

In Mexico, Luis can only make about $3.50 a day. That's not enough to live on. And he can't always find work. Sometimes they have nothing. The farms in Arizona pay much more. If only he can get to one.

Before he left Mexico, Luis prayed a lot. He prayed he would find a job in the United States. He prayed that no one would find out that he was illegal. He prayed that someday his family could join him. He prayed for a better life for all of them.

Now, sitting under the bush, Luis prays again. This time he only prays that he will not die. Suddenly the men hear an airplane. They can see it coming from the south. "It's the border patrol," whispers one of the men.

Nobody says a word. But the questions shout inside their heads. Will the border patrol see our footprints? Will they arrest us? Will they send us back to Mexico?

Luis pulls his feet up close. Will they see him through the bush?

The men can see the plane flying low. It is flying in circles. Then suddenly, it turns and flies away.

Luis watches it disappear. He feels his body relax. They will not be caught. Not now. Not yet.

The four men start walking again. They need water. Luis's head aches. His legs feel like rubber. He feels dizzy.

Luis suddenly feels the hot sand against his face. He has fallen. Sand is in his mouth and in his eyes.

"Get up!" one of the men says. But Luis can't get up. He is too weak.

"We don't want to leave you here," another
man says. "We cannot carry you. Get up!"

Luis gets to his hands and knees. He can't
stand up. The sand burns his hands. Slowly,
he starts to crawl.

Then one of his friends shouts, "The
highway! The highway! I can see it! Just over
there."

Two of the men pull on Luis's arms. They
pull him along. They are walking as fast as they
can. They have reached the highway. Just on
the other side is a canal—running with water!

Steady Work

It is two years later, 1986. Luis is in Arizona. He is tying grapevines to wires. The wires stretch between wood posts on a hillside.

Luis has done farm work all over Arizona. He has picked beans. He has picked oranges. Now he works for a farmer who grows grapes.

"This farmer treats us like slaves," says one of Luis's friends. He is working near Luis. "He does not even give us a place to sleep. I hate sleeping on the ground."

But Luis does not complain. For him, this job is another step toward making his dream come true. He is making $2.00 an hour. Not $3.50 a day. Soon he can send for Elena and the children.

Luis has almost enough money to pay for the trip. Elena and the children can't walk that terrible 40 miles across the desert. They will come by truck.

It is not legal to bring them here. If they are caught, they will be sent back.

Luis prays they will not be caught.

Luis dreams as he works. He will look for a steady job. Then he won't have to move so much. Maybe he and Elena can find a little house.

That summer, it happens. Luis finds a steady job. The job is at a farm in Chandler, Arizona.

The owner of the farm is Mr. Dobbs. He speaks a little Spanish. He doesn't even ask if Luis is American. He acts as if he doesn't want to know.

Mr. Dobbs pays Luis $2.50 an hour. He lets Luis stay in one of the farm sheds. It is dirty and small. The window and the hinges on the door are broken. There are cockroaches everywhere.

But Luis cleans the little shed. He fixes the window and the door. Now he has a place for his family.

The Second Miracle

Elena and the children are at the Mexican border town. They are very frightened. They get into the big truck with some other people. It is a furniture truck.

First, the drivers help the people in. Then they put furniture across the back. The truck looks like it is full of furniture.

There is not much air in the truck. It is hot. It is dark. The people can't see each other at all.

There is no room to move. No one is allowed to talk. Elena can only hear breathing. She feels fear around her.

Elena sits with her arms tightly around Carlos and María. "Don't cry," she whispers to them again and again. "We must be very quiet."

Later, the truck stops. This must be the border, Elena thinks. She can hear people talking outside. Will they get through? It is as quiet as death inside the truck. Elena can hardly hear anyone breathing. She, too, is holding her breath.

Then Elena hears the engine roar. The truck is moving again. Elena knows they are across the border.

The children fall asleep. But Elena stays awake. She is praying.

Hours later, the truck stops. Elena hears the back doors open. She hears people moving the furniture. Have they been caught?

"We are here," someone says. "In Chandler. In Arizona."

Then Elena feels the fresh air on her face. She takes a deep breath. Freedom! She wakes the children. "Come," she says. "You are safe now."

Some men help them out of the truck. Then Elena sees Luis. She wants to run to him. She sees the children running into his arms.

Elena falls down on her knees. "Thank you," she whispers into her folded hands. "Thank you. Thank you."

The End of the Dream

Luis goes on with his work. Elena takes care of the children. She plants flowers around the shed. She cooks delicious food. The children are happy.

Everything is perfect, except for one big worry. Will someone find out that Luis and Elena are illegal aliens? Will the border patrol come and arrest them? Luis tries not to think about it.

Luis is glad to get $2.50 an hour. But it is not enough. Now that his family is here, he needs more.

One day Luis finds out something that makes him angry. The legal workers are paid at least $3.75 an hour! Mr. Dobbs has to pay them that. It is a law in the United States. Then, after a few months, they get more. Some of the legal workers now make $5.00 an hour.

Luis cannot complain. If he does, Mr. Dobbs might report him to Immigration. He would be sent back to Mexico. Luis feels like a prisoner. He knows he will never make more than $2.50 an hour. His dream is not as bright as before.

Then one day, their worst fear comes true. Mr. Dobbs comes to their shed.

"You must leave," Mr. Dobbs says. "The border patrol is checking all the farms for illegals. I know you're from Mexico. I wasn't supposed to hire you. If they find you here, I'll be in big trouble."

Mr. Dobbs shakes his head sadly. "I'm sorry, Luis. You're a good worker. But you have to be out of here by tomorrow."

"Where will we go?" asks Luis.

"Go down to the immigration office," says Mr. Dobbs. "I hear there is something called Amnesty."

"What does that mean?" asks Luis.

"I'm not sure exactly. I think if you've been in the States for a while, you can stay. You can work and live here. You get a work permit," says Mr. Dobbs.

"What about my family?" asks Luis. "They have only been here a year."

"I don't know about that," says Mr. Dobbs. "They might have to go back."

Mr. Dobbs walks away. Then he turns back. "Listen, Luis," he says. "If they give you a work permit, you come back here. I'll hire you as a legal worker." He smiles and points at Elena and the children. "Then you can send money back to them in Mexico."

Families Belong Together

Luis and Elena can't sleep that night. "I don't want to go back to Mexico," says Elena.

"I don't want to stay here without you," says Luis. "But there is no work for me in Mexico." He puts his head in his hands. "What are we going to do?"

The next day they go to the immigration office downtown. They take Carlos and María with them. They want to be together, whatever happens.

The office is crowded with people. Most of them are from Mexico. Most of them look scared.

Luis takes a number and sits down with his family. Luis has time to think. This may be the last time we are safely together. Will the family be sent back today? Can I stay and work? Or will we all be sent back?

Luis hears his number called. He and Elena go up to the desk. The children follow. The officer behind the desk is a large man. He looks at Luis.

Luis thinks of many lies he could tell. But he knows he must tell the truth. He tells the man about walking across "the Devil's Highway." He tells of paying a lot of money to get his family here. He tells of working on many different farms. He does not tell the names of the farmers.

The officer nods. Then he says, "Fill out these forms. You can stay and work. You must pay taxes. This is the Amnesty program. You can stay in the United States."

The officer gives Luis the papers. "We know things have been hard for you. We want you to be able to work for fair pay," he says.

"What about my family?" asks Luis. His son leans against him. María sits in Elena's lap.

The man looks through some papers. Then he looks at Elena and the children. Is he frowning?

Oh no, thinks Luis. I have lost them. They will have to go back to Mexico. This is worse than "the Devil's Highway." Luis feels like he is dying. But this time, not of thirst.

The officer smiles at Elena and the children. "We are not in the business of breaking up families. They can stay where they belong. With you."

Luis takes a deep breath. He lets it out slowly. He turns to look at Elena. But she is not in the chair. Elena is on her knees. In English she says, "Thank you."

Luis knows she is not saying this to the officer.

Elena's prayers have been answered.

Amnesty means "all is forgiven." The Amnesty program was created by the Immigration Reform and Control Act of 1986 (IRCA). The program allowed some illegal aliens to become legal residents of the United States. They had to register with the immigration office. They also had to meet certain requirements.

The program's deadline for applying for amnesty was in 1988. Illegal aliens can no longer become legal residents through the program.

Powerful Medicine

Emergency Room

Dr. Cole has another cup of coffee. He is very tired this Saturday. The hospital emergency room is always busy on Saturdays. There are so many emergencies. So many accidents.

Dan Cole has been a doctor for only one year. But today it feels like a century. He yawns and rubs his eyes. He is so sleepy.

Dr. Cole is drinking his coffee. Suddenly, he hears his name on the loudspeaker. "Dr. Cole to the emergency room."

The doctor runs down the hall. He sees a woman in a long, gray robe. She has a scarf around her head. It almost hides her eyes. She is holding a small boy in her arms. The boy is screaming and crying.

A nurse pushes a cart up next to the woman. "Please," the nurse says. "Let the boy lie down here."

But the woman will not put him on the cart. She holds him tightly in her arms.

Dr. Cole and the nurse step away from the woman. They talk quietly.

"Dr. Cole," the nurse says. "She won't let us look at the boy."

"What happened?" asks the doctor.

"He fell off a swing in the park and hit his head," says the nurse. She looks at the little boy. "For a while he was knocked out. Someone in the park called an ambulance."

"Is this woman his mother?" asks Dr. Cole.

"Yes," answers the nurse.

"Do you know their names?" Dr. Cole asks. The nurse looks at the clipboard she is carrying. "The boy's name is Timur Taraki."

Dr. Cole walks over to the boy and his mother. He smiles and asks, "Mrs. Taraki, do you speak English?"

The woman only shakes her head.

Oh, no, thinks Dr. Cole. "What country is she from?" he asks the nurse.

"The ambulance driver said she is from Afghanistan," the nurse says.

Dr. Cole looks surprised. "How does the ambulance driver know?" he asks.

"He speaks the same language," says the nurse. "He was talking with the mother when they brought the boy in. He helped fill out the papers. I think he is also Afghan."

"That was very lucky," says Dr. Cole.

The nurse nods. "Yes, it's lucky he was on duty," she says.

Dr. Cole turns to the woman. He points to his own chest. "I am a doctor," he says slowly. He speaks loudly. "I want to help you." He holds out his arms. "Please let me look at your child." He places his hand on the cart. "Put him here," he says.

At last, the woman puts the boy on the cart. But she holds his hand. The boy keeps crying.

Dr. Cole looks at the little boy's eyes. They don't look right. They are out of focus. Timur is very pale. Dr. Cole feels the big lump on the boy's head. "We will have to x-ray him," he says.

The nurse pushes the cart. They start into the x-ray room. The woman looks around. She looks afraid. "No!" she shouts. She tries to take the boy from the cart. When they hold her back she keeps shouting "No! No! No!"

Dr. Cole feels his anger growing. At least she knows one English word, he thinks. This woman is foolish. Her son needs to be x-rayed. He needs to stay in the hospital. Doesn't she see that bump on his head?

"Please," Dr. Cole says. He is so tired. His head is aching. "Just let me help the boy."

The woman suddenly runs from the room. Dr. Cole and the nurse are too surprised to move. Then the nurse chases after the woman.

A few minutes later, the nurse comes back. "She's gone."

"Gone where?" asks Dr. Cole.

"I didn't see where. I'm sorry," the nurse says.

Dr. Cole looks down at the boy. Timur is moaning. "Let's get this kid to x-ray," says Dr. Cole. "Someone else will have to find his parents."

The Family

Fara runs from the hospital. She must get her husband, Ahmad. Those people are trying to take their son. Ahmad will know what to do.

She runs out onto the sidewalk. There is a taxi waiting in front of the hospital. Slowly, Fara tells the driver her address. She can say her address in English. She learned it when they first came to this country.

I must get Ahmad, Fara thinks. I must get home. What will they do to him? Timur might die in that American hospital.

Fara pays the cab driver. Then she runs into the house.

"Ahmad!" she shouts. "They have taken our child!"

The family gathers around Fara. She tells them what happened.

Ahmad looks very angry as his wife speaks. "My son in the hospital? No!" he says. "Hospitals are places where people die. Timur needs to be with his family! We must go to him."

Fara tells Ahmad it's the hospital near the park. Ahmad and his three brothers hurry out the door. Fara watches them go. She is afraid.

The Hospital Visit

The nurse on the children's floor looks up. She smiles when she sees the four Afghan men. They look grand with their dark beards. One wears cloth wrapped around his head in a turban.

"You must be here to see Timur," she says. "He's right in here."

The little boy is crying softly. He cries louder when he sees his father and uncles. One of the men takes Timur in his arms.

The nurse leaves them alone. It's nice that Timur's family has come, she thinks.

A few minutes later, the nurse looks up. The door to Timur's room is closed. But she no longer hears voices. That's strange, she thinks. Something is wrong. She walks over and looks into the room.

It is empty! The window is open. The men are gone.

So is Timur.

Kidnapped

Dr. Cole is leaving the hospital. He hears his name again on the loudspeaker. He is so tired he can hardly see. What now, he wonders? The nurse tells him that the Afghan boy is missing. Little Timur has been taken by a group of men.

"Find that ambulance driver!" Dr. Cole shouts. "The one who brought him in. We're going to need him."

"He's here," says a nurse. "He just came in. We've called the police."

A young man with a dark beard follows the nurse. He is wearing a white uniform. "I am Mohammad," he says. "What can I do?"

"Do you know the Taraki family?" Dr. Cole asks.

"I only met Mrs. Taraki today," Mohammad says. "She was afraid of coming to the hospital."

"Do you know that Timur has been kidnapped?" asks Dr. Cole.

"Yes. The nurses told me," says Mohammad. "But I am not surprised. The Tarakis are from a small village in Afghanistan. People there would not trust hospitals."

"Now they really won't trust us," says Dr. Cole. "How can we tell them that their son has been taken?" He shakes his head.

The police arrive.

"Doctor," says Mohammad. "You don't have to worry. I can tell you where the boy is. His father has taken him home. I am sure of it."

"They just walked out with him?" asks Dr. Cole. He can hardly believe it. How can the Tarakis be so foolish, he thinks? Their child could die. "They have no right to do that," he says.

"But they think you have no right to keep the boy," says Mohammad quietly. "Come, I'll take you to them. I can find their house."

Dr. Cole walks toward the police. "I must tell them where . . ." he starts to say.

But Mohammad stops him. "It would be better not to take the police," he says. "That would make the family more afraid."

The Healer

Dr. Cole and Mohammad walk up to the Tarakis' house. A man opens the door. He doesn't smile. He stares at Dr. Cole from under his turban.

Then three other men join the man at the door. They all look very serious. Their dark eyes are full of anger.

Dr. Cole feels his heart beat faster. He swallows hard. He is frightened.

Then one of the men speaks.

"What did he say?" Dr. Cole asks Mohammad.

"He said, 'Welcome. May God bring you here always,'" Mohammad says.

"What?" Dr. Cole can't believe it. "They think I'm going to hurt their son? But they welcome me?"

Mohammad grins. "It is our way," he says. "We always welcome a stranger. Even if he is an enemy."

Mohammad explains to the family why Dr. Cole has come.

The men bring Dr. Cole into the living room. Timur is lying on the couch. He is smiling. This is the first time Dr. Cole has seen him smile.

Timur's mother is sitting on one side of him. On the other side sits an old woman. She wears a black robe and scarf. She is saying the same words again and again. Her voice is low and musical.

Dr. Cole looks closely at Timur. He notices the boy's eyes. They are clear and focused. Then Dr. Cole looks more closely. Timur's skin color is healthier than before. His cheeks are pinker. There is a warm cloth on the place where he hit his head.

The room smells spicy. It is the smell of cinnamon. And there is something else sharp and sweet in the air.

Timur is happy and wide awake. That is good.

"May I look at his head?" asks Dr. Cole.

Mohammad translates the question. The men speak together. Ahmad nods. Dr. Cole lifts the cloth. The lump is much smaller now.

"Who is Timur's father?" Dr. Cole asks.

Mohammed points out Ahmad.

"Why did you take Timur from the hospital?" Dr. Cole asks.

Mohammed repeats Ahmad's answer. "Because in the hospital you treat only the body. We believe that there are three locations of health. Body, mind, and soul. The soul and mind are not separate from the body. All work together."

Dr. Cole looks at Timur's father. He no longer sees anger in Ahmad's face. Ahmad speaks quietly.

"A child belongs with his family," says Ahmad. Mohammad translates for Dr. Cole. "And we have a healer here." Ahmad points to the old woman. "She knows about herbs. She knows that the fragrance of certain things can heal. See how the boy looks better?"

Dr. Cole agrees that Timur does look better. "But sometimes the bone of the skull is cracked," he says. "Or the brain is bruised. This can be very serious. We want to keep him in the hospital. To make sure he is all right."

Mohammad translates Dr. Cole's words.

Ahmad frowns. "In our country, many people go to the hospital and do not return. They die there."

"Don't people also die at home?" asks Dr. Cole. "Sometimes they are just too sick to live." He is silent for a while. Then he says, "In the hospital we can save lives, too."

Ahmad nods. "You are right," he says. "But children need to be with their family. That

helps them get well. Love is the most powerful medicine."

This man is very wise, thinks Dr. Cole. He is reminding me of important things. "Parents can stay with their child in the hospital," says Dr. Cole. "You may stay in the same room with Timur. Please bring him back to the hospital. We need to watch him for one night. If everything is all right, he can come home tomorrow."

"May Timur's grandmother come, too?" asks Ahmad. "She is his healer."

Dr. Cole smiles. "I would very much like her to come."

The old woman says something to Dr. Cole. Mohammad grins. "She says you look like you have a headache."

"She is right," says Dr. Cole. He puts his hand to his head.

"She says to sit down. She will cure it," says Mohammad.

Dr. Cole smiles. I'll give the grandmother a chance, he thinks. But what I really want is an aspirin.

He sits in a big chair. The old woman closes his eyes with her cool fingers. She begins to rub his temples. She rubs in something that smells sweet. Her hands are like the wings of birds. On his head, his neck, his face. Then the ache is gone.

"She says you need to go home and sleep," says Mohammad.

"Tell her I will do that," says Dr. Cole. Then he looks into her eyes. "As soon as Timur is back at the hospital."

Ahmad speaks. Mohammad translates.

"He says he will take Timur back to the hospital. He thanks you."

Dr. Cole feels relaxed and sleepy. "How did the old lady do that?" he asks Mohammad.

Mohammad smiles and answers, "Old wisdom."

New
Birth on
Pike Street

Pike Street in Black and White

It is Sunday. Jong sits on the steps outside his apartment building. His neighbor, Sasha, sits next to him. "This whole place stinks," Jong says.

Sasha nods. "It is not what I expected," he says. "When I came here from Russia, I thought things would be different."

Jong leans back on the dirty, broken
concrete. It feels hard against his old bones.
He stares at the apartment building across
the street. It is just like his. The front of it is
dirty gray. He sees the shabby steps. Each
apartment building has shabby steps. Each
building is run-down and ugly. Inside, the
apartments are no better, Jong thinks. Outside,
they smell of garbage. Inside, they smell of
bathrooms.

Kids are playing on the cracked sidewalks. Their clothes are old. A rusty bicycle leans against a wall. The bicycle has only one wheel. Jong looks at the wall. Someone has painted a bad word in black spray paint.

"Pike Street is not the American dream. That is for sure," says Sasha. "Our landlord is a crook. He is never going to fix things up. We asked him to repair our stove and broken window. Months have gone by. But nothing is fixed."

Sasha goes on. "I have painted all my walls. I work as a painter, you know. My boss gave me some leftover paint. So the landlord didn't even have to pay for the paint."

They see a young woman walking slowly up the street. She's very pregnant. "Look, here comes our new neighbor," Jong says. "She and her husband are from Puerto Rico. They just moved into our building. Do you know her?"

"Yes," says Sasha. "We met last week." He thinks for a minute. "Her name is María. Her husband's name is Esteban."

María walks to the steps. She looks up at Jong and Sasha. "Hello," she says. She puts her grocery bag on the step.

"Are you settling in all right?" asks Sasha.

"Yes," says María. She wrinkles her nose. She sniffs the air. "Something smells bad," she says.

"That's just what we were saying," Jong says.

He looks at María. Her baby will be born very soon. Jong is sad that the baby must live on such an ugly street.

Jong stares out at Pike Street. Cigarette butts litter the steps. There are big holes in the sidewalk. The holes are full of garbage. One of these holes is right in front of their steps. There's trash and broken glass everywhere. What a terrible place for a child, Jong thinks.

"When I came here from Korea, I was so happy," Jong says. "I thought America would be beautiful. I thought it would be a dream come true."

"I thought the same thing," Sasha says. "In pictures and movies, the streets were beautiful. They were lined with flowers and trees." He looks at the door. The paint is peeling off it. "The pictures showed everything clean and nice."

"Imagine taking a picture of Pike Street," says Sasha. "Even if you used color film, the pictures would look black and white."

"No," says Jong. "They would be gray."

"And nobody cares," says Sasha. He shakes his head.

"I care," says María.

María picks up her grocery bag. She sighs and goes into the building.

María's Flowers

The next afternoon Jong is walking home from work. He turns onto Pike Street. Right away he sees that something is different.

The street is still dirty. There is still trash everywhere. But the steps leading up to his apartment are swept clean.

On each step is a small flower pot. Each pot has a plant with bright red flowers. The flowers are so beautiful and simple. Jong smiles as he enters the building.

"Who put the flowers on the step?" Jong asks his wife Sung.

"I think it was that young woman from Puerto Rico," Sung says.

Jong falls asleep that night thinking of the flowers. He feels happy. What a difference a few pots of flowers can make!

The next morning he walks out the door smiling. He looks down to see the flowers.

He does see them. They are smashed all over the steps. The pots are broken into tiny pieces. Someone stepped on the flowers and crushed them. Jong can't believe it.

He just stands there. He doesn't know what to do. He feels helpless.

Then he hears the door open. Jong turns. María is standing in the doorway.

María stares at the broken pots. Tears come to her eyes. "Oh, no," she cries. "My flowers." She turns and runs back to her apartment.

The Tree

Jong goes to work with a heavy heart. He feels sick. He keeps thinking of the smashed flowers. He makes fists with his hands. But he has nothing to hit.

When he goes home for lunch, Sung says, "María has gone to the hospital. The baby is coming."

Jong works hard all afternoon. He thinks hard, too. He decides what he will do.

After work, he walks to the bank. He takes out money. It is money he has been saving for a new refrigerator. Then he takes the bus to a garden shop. There they sell trees and flowers.

People stare at Jong when he gets back on the bus. He is carrying a tree. It is not a very big tree. It is in a five-gallon bucket. He has a large bag with some flower pots in it. There also are some small plants with red flowers in the bag. He bought a shovel, too.

It is hard walking the two blocks from the bus stop. Jong carries the tree in one arm. It rises four feet above his head. The bag and shovel are in his other hand.

He does not go up to his apartment. He goes right to work.

Sasha comes home from work. He finds Jong digging. Jong is digging the soil at the bottom of the hole in the sidewalk. He has removed all the garbage from the hole. It is piled beside the steps.

Sasha goes into the apartment building. He comes back out with a garbage bag. He puts the garbage inside.

Jong plants his tree. He works quickly. Then he puts the plants in the pots.

Sasha gets a broom. He sweeps the sidewalk. He sweeps the steps.

"One more thing," says Jong. He gets a bucket of water. He pours it on the steps. Sasha sweeps the water away.

Sasha and Jong stand and look at their steps. "Now María's baby will have a clean place to come home to," Jong says.

"How will you protect the tree and the flowers?" asks Sasha. "The last ones were ruined. Whoever did it will come back. You can be sure of that."

"Whoever it is will have to deal with me," says Jong.

After dark, Jong comes down from his
apartment. He has a pillow and blanket. He
sits at the top of the steps. He pulls the blanket
around himself and leans back on the pillow.

The Plant Smashers

It is the middle of the night. Jong is very sleepy. He just dozes off when he hears voices. Four teenage boys are walking up the street. They stop by the tree. "Hey Rico," says one of them. "Want to climb a tree?" They all laugh. One of them reaches out and shakes the tree.

Jong stands up. "What is so funny?" he asks. He tries to sound brave.

"Is this your tree?" asks one of them.

"Stop it, Mick," says the one called Rico.

"The tree belongs to everyone on this street," Jong says.

"This street belongs to us," the biggest boy says. "And nobody else."

"Then the tree belongs to you," says Jong.

"That's stupid," says the short boy.

The boy named Rico pushes him. "What's stupid about it, Mick?" he asks. "We never had a tree here before."

"It's yours," says Jong. "But somebody has to watch it." He looks at the boys. "To watch and see that nobody hurts it."

"I still say it's stupid," says Mick.

"I say *you're* stupid," says Rico. "Hey, a tree on Pike Street. That's cool." He walks up the steps. "Flowers, too, huh?"

"I thought we got rid of these last night," says Mick in a loud whisper.

Jong stands very still as they climb the steps. Is Rico making fun of him? He knows who they are. They are the boys who ruined María's flowers. His heart is beating very fast.

"Are these our flowers, too?" asks Rico.

What should I do, Jong wonders? If I say yes, will they smash the flower pots again? If I say no, will they hurt me? "Yes, they are yours," he says quietly.

Then he says, "There is a young woman in this building. Tonight she is having a baby." Jong swallows. These are tough kids. Will they understand? "I think this baby should have a home with a tree and flowers."

"Old man, you're crazy," says Mick.

"Shut up, Mick," says Rico. He turns to Jong. "Did you put these here?"

"Yes," says Jong.

"Are you guarding them?" asks Rico.

"Yes," says Jong. "But I need help. I can't sleep out here every night."

Rico slaps Jong on the back. "You don't have to worry, old man," he says. "We will guard this tree. You said it was ours."

Rico turns to his friends. "If any of you see anyone touch this tree, tell them this." He bends his arm and points to the muscle. "They will have to answer to me."

Two days later, Esteban brings María home. She is holding their new baby daughter.

María sees the tree. She sees the flowers. "Oh, how lovely," she says. She lifts the baby up. "Look, little Carmen," she says. "See how beautiful your home is?" She smiles. Her smile is worth everything to Jong.

Barn Raising

Things are changing on Pike Street. More flowers are on front steps. Families come out together. They clean up the trash. They wash down the sidewalks. Someone even plants flowers under Jong's tree.

Sasha comes home one day with a can of paint. He looks at the peeling paint on the building door. He scrapes it off. Then he paints the door green.

Jong sees Sasha across the street. He is painting the door. Jong goes over. "Are you the neighborhood painter?"

"I guess so," says Sasha. "I offered to do it." Sasha stops painting. "Then my wife got the idea to have a meeting." He hands Jong a piece of paper.

Jong looks at the paper. He can't read it. "What kind of meeting?" he asks.

"A neighborhood meeting," says Sasha. "A Pike Street meeting."

"What for?" asks Jong.

"To find out what people can do," says Sasha. "What we can all do together to improve Pike Street."

Sasha sits down to explain. "My wife read a book about the first immigration to the United States. Most of the people were farmers. Everyone worked together. When someone needed a barn, everyone helped build it. It was called a 'barn raising.' My wife thinks we could have kind of a barn raising here. Right here on Pike Street."

"We don't need a barn," Jong says.

"But we do need to improve the place," says Sasha. "You know Mr. Olivas who lives in the next building? I found out that he works for a plumber. Maybe he could help us fix broken pipes. Everyone can do something. It just takes caring."

Jong smiles at Sasha. "Caring does make a difference," he says. He looks up and down Pike Street. He looks at the flowers, at the tree, and the clean, swept sidewalks.

"Young María was the first to say 'I care,'" says Jong. "Now look at Pike Street. We all care."

About the Author

Rosanne Keller is a writer who lives in St. Joseph, Minnesota. She has taught English as a second language (ESL) and writing. She has taught classes on how literacy affects people. She also has worked as a flagger on a road construction crew.

Ms. Keller makes sculpture and loves to travel. She often writes about the places she visits. Her articles and stories have appeared in many publications. New Readers Press has published several books written by Ms. Keller for ESL learners and adult new readers.

In this book's companion volume, *The Orange Grove and Other Stories,* you can read four more stories about people with some very human problems to solve. Read-along tapes are available to add another level of learning and enjoyment.